Baby's First
BANK
HEIST

Jim Whalley

illustrated by
Stephen Collins

BLOOMSBURY
CHILDREN'S BOOKS

NEW YORK LONDON OXFORD NEW DELHI SYDNEY

BLOOMSBURY CHILDREN'S BOOKS
Bloomsbury Publishing Inc., part of Bloomsbury Publishing Plc
1385 Broadway, New York, NY 10018

BLOOMSBURY, BLOOMSBURY CHILDREN'S BOOKS, and the Diana logo are trademarks of Bloomsbury Publishing Plc

First published in Great Britain in June 2018 by Bloomsbury Publishing Plc
Published in the United States of America in March 2019 by Bloomsbury Children's Books

Text copyright © 2018 by Jim Whalley
Illustrations copyright © 2018 by Stephen Collins

Bloomsbury books may be purchased for business or promotional use. For information on bulk purchases please contact Macmillan Corporate and Premium Sales Department at specialmarkets@macmillan.com

Library of Congress Cataloging-in-Publication Data
LCCN 2018011658 (hardcover) | LCCN 2018018257 (e-book)
ISBN 978-1-5476-0062-5 (hardcover) • ISBN 978-1-5476-0063-2 (e-book) • ISBN 978-1-5476-0064-9 (e-PDF)

Art created with gouache and ink on paper, then scanned and edited in Photoshop
Typeset in Bookman Old Style
Book design by Stephanie Amster
Printed in China by Leo Paper Products, Heshan, Guangdong
2 4 6 8 10 9 7 5 3 1

All papers used by Bloomsbury Publishing Plc are natural, recyclable products made from wood grown in well-managed forests. The manufacturing processes conform to the environmental regulations of the country of origin.

To find out more about our authors and books visit www.bloomsbury.com
and sign up for our newsletters.

JW: For Fletch & Charlie, partners in crime
SC: For Frank, George & Meg, with all my love

Baby Frank loved animals,
and yet he could not get
his mom and dad to understand
how much he'd like a pet.

It didn't matter what it was—
a dog, a cat, or rabbit—
if Frank saw fur while out on walks,
he'd lunge and try to grab it.

And though each night at story time,
young Frank would always choose
books involving birds and beasts,
from ducks to kangaroos,

his parents would not change their minds.
His mom said, "You're not ready."
"AND they cost too much," said Dad.
"Be happy with your teddy."

Frank tried to think of all the ways
a pet could be obtained.
He was sure that he could steal one,
but the problem still remained . . .

of how he was supposed to find
the money he would need
to buy his newfound furry friend
its bedding, bowl, and feed.

Out shopping with his mom one day,
the answer came to Frank.
"There really is no other choice—
I'll have to rob a bank."

With Mom stuck waiting in a line,
he knew the time was right . . .

so Frank put on a bandit mask
and disappeared from sight.

Past every camera,
gate, and guard,

the baby
crawled unseen.

There were no bars

or laser beams

he couldn't fit between.

Quick as a flash, he found the vault,
and scooped up all the loot.
He swiftly stuffed the bills and coins
inside his onesie suit.

Then back to Mom he scampered and sat down without a fuss.
Nobody tried to stop him as he went home on the bus.

Late that night, Frank crept downstairs
and turned on the computer.
He started searching animals
to check which ones were cuter.

He knew he wanted
something small
but not a boring mouse,
and so it was that Frank received . . .

. . . a meerkat at his house!

He snuck his pet up to his room and kept it out of sight,
and practiced looking after her, to show he'd do it right.

The meerkat was a great success, and little Frank adored it . . .

but pretty soon he wanted more—why not? He could afford it.

First a dog, and then a pig, two aardvarks, and a cat
were smuggled up into his room. He should have stopped at that.

There were leopards in his cupboards and a beaver in the bath.

And Frank was **really** struggling to hide his new giraffe.

It all went wrong one afternoon
when Mom called out and said,
"Don't be alarmed
but I just found . . .

...a **rhino** in our shed."

It took her some detective work
to find out Frank's deceit . . .

stacks of bills, a bandit mask,
and piles of named receipts.

Mom showed her clues to Dad
and said it was her firm belief,
"Our baby wanted pets so much
he's turned into . . .

a thief!"

Once Frank could see how sad they were, he quickly understood that stealing things was very wrong. From now on he'd be good.

Frank's parents took him to the bank and told them of the theft. The bank asked for their money, but there wasn't any left.

The family went home to their pets
and wondered what to do.

Until at last Dad had a thought . . .

"Let's open up a zoo."

By selling tickets at the door, they soon began to save.
Frank tried his best to lend a hand and show he could behave.

He served his time without a doubt and though still on all fours,
it didn't stop him cleaning up and even leading tours.

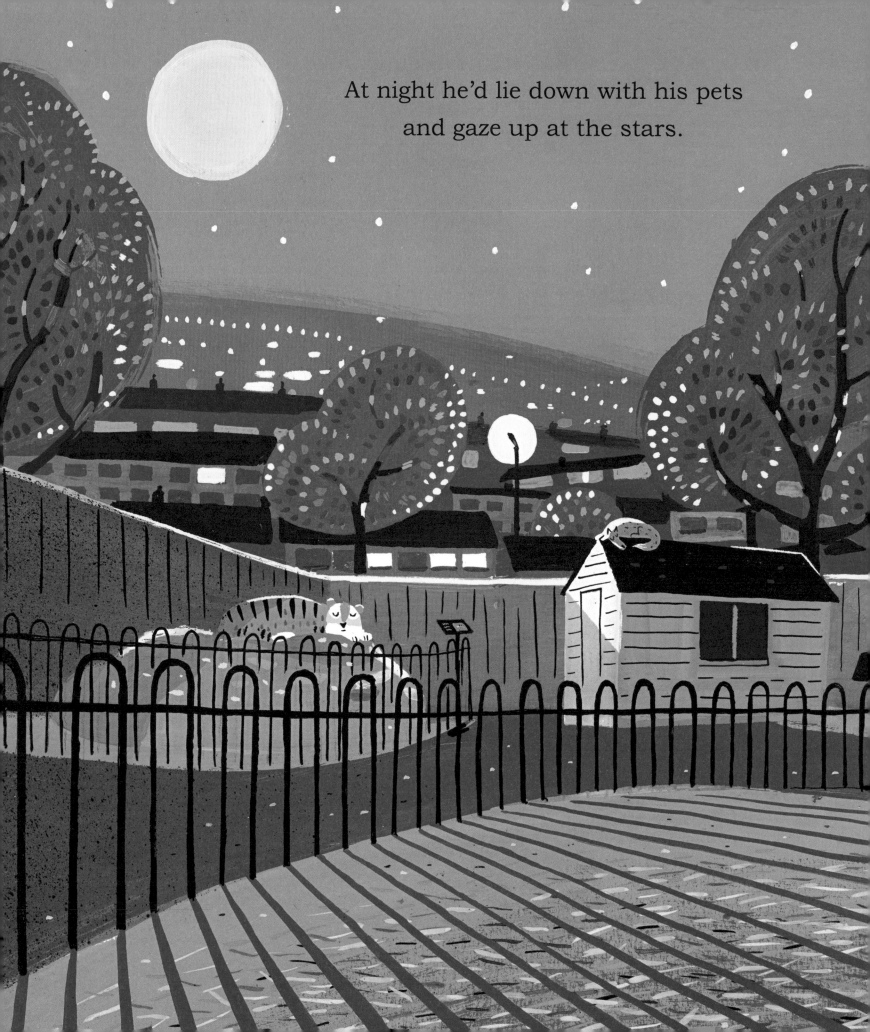

At night he'd lie down with his pets
and gaze up at the stars.

Baby Frank had
got his way . . .

He was happy **behind bars.**